THE SHY LITTLE KITTEN

Adapted from the beloved Little Golden Book
written by Cathleen Schurr and illustrated by Gustaf Tenggren

By Kristen Depken
Illustrated by Sue DiCicco

Random House New York

One mama cat.

Six little kittens.

Black-and-white.

One has stripes.

Down the ladder.

6

Jump, jump, jump!

Onto the grass.
Roll, roll, roll!

The little striped kitten
is very shy.

Pop!

A chubby mole!

They go
for a walk.

Green frog.
Big mouth!

The mole and the kitten
laugh and laugh.

Bounce, bounce!
A shaggy puppy!

Where is the mama cat?

The shaggy puppy knows!

"Woof, woof!"

A red squirrel!

"Chee, chee, chee!"

Down the hill.

Hop, hop, hop!
Across the brook.

Onto the farm.

Mama cat!

One, two, three, four,
five, six little kittens.

Picnic time
on the farm!

Seeds for the chickens and ducks.

Carrots for the rabbits.

Mash for the pigs.

Berries and milk
for the little
kittens!

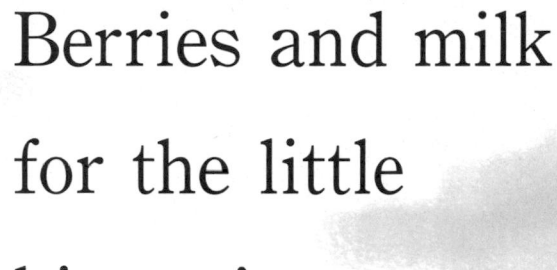

Uh-oh.

PLOP!

PLOP!

SPLASH!

30

All the animals
laugh and laugh.

Best day ever!